India
the Moonstone
Fairy

For Danni who loves fairies

Special thanks to
Narinder Dhami

No part of this work may be reproduced, stored in a
retrieval system, or transmitted in any form or by any
means, electronic, mechanical, photocopying, recording, or otherwise,
without written permission of the publisher. For information
regarding permission, write to Working Partners Limited,
1 Albion Place, London, W6 0QT, United Kingdom.

ISBN-10: 0-545-01188-4
ISBN-13: 978-0-545-01188-4

12 11 10 9 8 7 6 5 4 3 2 1   7 8 9 10 11 12/0

Printed in the U.S.A.   40

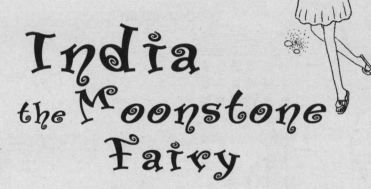

India
the Moonstone
Fairy

by Daisy Meadows
illustrated by Georgie Ripper

SCHOLASTIC INC.

New York   Toronto   London   Auckland   Sydney
Mexico City   New Delhi   Hong Kong   Buenos Aires

The Fairyland Palace

Adventure Playground

Tippington Manor

Tippington Town

The Tall Toy Store

Fountain

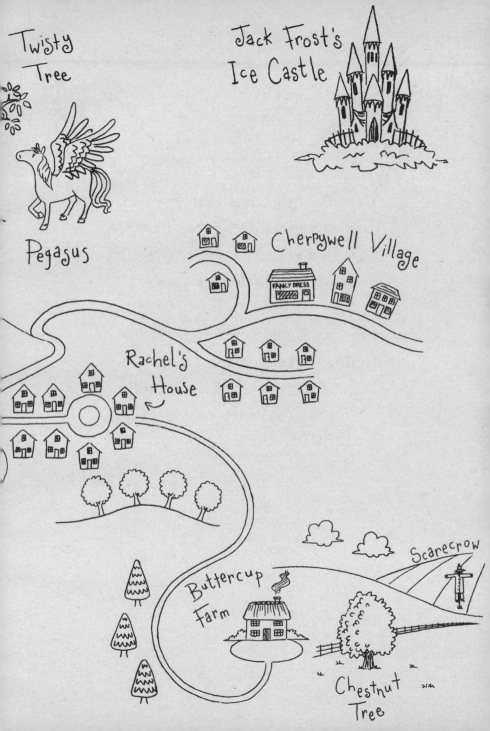

By frosty magic I cast away
These seven jewels with their fiery rays,
So their magic powers will not be felt
And my icy castle shall not melt.

The fairies may search high and low
To find the gems and take them home.
But I will send my goblin guards
To make the fairies' mission hard.

Contents

A Nasty Nightmare

"Kirsty, help!" Rachel Walker shouted. "The goblins are going to get me!"

Breathing hard, Rachel glanced behind her. She was running as fast as she could, but the green goblins were getting closer and closer. They were grinning nastily, showing their pointed teeth. Now one of

them had grabbed Rachel by the
shoulder and was shaking her —

"Rachel?" Kirsty Tate was leaning
over her friend's bed, trying to awaken
her. "Wake up! You're having a
nightmare."

Rachel sat up in bed. "What time is
it?" she asked. "I had a dream that there
were horrible goblins chasing me and I
couldn't get away."

"It's seven thirty," Kirsty replied, sitting on the edge of the bed. "Why were the goblins after you in your dream?"

Rachel frowned. "I can't remember," she said, sighing. "But you know what, Kirsty? I have a funny feeling that Jack Frost might be causing trouble again!"

Kirsty eyes opened wide. "Do you really think so?" She gasped. "Then maybe our fairy friends need our help!"

Rachel and Kirsty shared a magical secret. They had become friends with the fairies! Whenever there was a problem in Fairyland, Kirsty and Rachel were asked to help.

The fairies' biggest enemy was Jack Frost. He and his mean goblins were always causing problems. Not long ago, Jack Frost had mixed up all the weather in Fairyland. But luckily, Kirsty and Rachel had come to the rescue.

"We'll have to keep our eyes open," Rachel agreed. "If the fairies need our help, they'll let us know somehow."

Kirsty nodded. "Well, it's only the beginning of our school break, and I'm staying with you for the whole week," she pointed out. "So we have lots of time."

Before Rachel could reply, she felt a gentle tug at her neck. Both she and Kirsty jumped.

"What was that?" Kirsty asked.

Rachel looked at her friend. "You felt it, too?" Rachel looked down and gasped. The locket around her neck was glowing! "Look, Kirsty!" she cried. "Your locket is glowing, too!"

Rachel and Kirsty took a closer look at their necklaces. Rachel was right! The lockets were glowing with a faint pink light.

After helping the Weather Fairies stop Jack Frost from mixing up the weather in Fairyland, Rachel and Kirsty had each been given a beautiful locket. The lockets were filled with fairy dust, and the girls wore them every day. But they had never glowed like this before! What could it mean? There was only one way to find out. The girls were pretty sure that another fairy adventure wasn't far away!

"Let's open them, Rachel," Kirsty whispered.

Holding their breath, both girls slowly pried open their lockets.

Immediately, a glittering shower of multicolored fairy dust burst from both lockets. It swirled around the girls, wrapping them in a cloud of sparkles and lifting them off their feet.

Fairy News

After a minute or two, the sparkles began to fade. Rachel and Kirsty felt their feet lightly touch the ground. They blinked a few times and looked around.

"Kirsty, we're in Fairyland!" Rachel gasped.

"In our pajamas!" Kirsty added.

The girls were fairy-size and had

glittering fairy wings on their backs!
They were standing in the golden Great
Hall of the fairy palace. King Oberon,
Queen Titania, and a small crowd of
fairies stood in front of them. The girls
noticed that all of the fairies looked very
worried.

Queen Titania stepped forward.
"Welcome back, girls," she said with a
smile. "I hope you don't mind us
bringing you here without warning."

"Of course not," Rachel said quickly.

"You have been such good friends to us in the past," the queen went on. "We were hoping you might be able to help us again. I'm afraid that we are in trouble."

"What's wrong?" asked Kirsty.

"Let me explain," the queen replied sadly. "Every year, at Halloween, we have a huge celebration in Fairyland. That's when all the fairies recharge their fairy magic for another year."

"Every fairy in Fairyland parades around the Grand Square," King Oberon added. "Then they all march into the palace, where Queen Titania's crown rests upon a velvet pillow."

"It sounds wonderful," Rachel said. She hoped that she and Kirsty would be allowed to watch the parade one day.

Queen Titania nodded. "It is," she replied. "And my crown is a very important part of fairy magic. It contains seven beautiful jewels. A sparkling fountain of fairy dust pours from each of the seven jewels, and they join together to form a great, glittering rainbow."

Kirsty and Rachel listened carefully, their eyes wide. "What happens then?" Kirsty asked.

"Each fairy must recharge her wand by dipping it in the rainbow," the queen explained. "Then she will be able to perform magic for another year."

The king shook his head sadly. "But now Jack Frost has ended all that," he said, sighing. "Two nights ago, he crept into the palace and stole the seven jewels from Queen Titania's crown!"

"Oh, no!" Rachel and Kirsty exclaimed together.

"Our special celebration is only a week away," the queen went on, looking worried. "So the fairies' magic is already running low."

"The jewels must be returned to the
crown before the Jewel Fairies run out of
magic completely!" King Oberon added.

"Does this mean that there will be no
magic at all left in Fairyland?" asked
Kirsty anxiously.

"Not exactly," the queen replied.
"Fairy magic is more complicated than
that. Some magic, like Weather Magic
and Rainbow Magic, isn't controlled

by the jewels."

"But the jewels do
control some of
the most
important kinds of
fairy magic,"
the king added.
"They are in charge

of things like flying, wishes, and sweet dreams. Some people have already started to have nightmares!"

Rachel nodded, thinking about her own scary dream. "We have to get the jewels back!" she said firmly.

"Where is Jack Frost now?" Kirsty asked. "Did he

take the jewels to his ice castle?"

The queen shook her head. "Jack Frost doesn't have the jewels anymore," she said. "Come with us. We will show you what happened."

Rachel and Kirsty followed the fairies outside to the beautiful palace gardens. They stopped next to the golden pool. Its surface was as clear and smooth as glass.

"Watch," Queen Titania said softly, waving her wand over the water.

Immediately, tiny ripples spread across the surface of the pool. The ripples grew bigger and bigger, and a picture slowly appeared in the water.

"It's Jack Frost!" Rachel cried. Tall, thin Jack Frost stood in front of Queen Titania's golden crown. The seven magic jewels glittered as streams of magic dust poured from them. Laughing, Jack Frost thrust his wand into the magic rainbow, where it glowed like fire. "He is recharging his magic," King Oberon explained.

Kirsty and Rachel watched in dismay as Jack Frost pulled the sparkling gems out of the crown. He waved his wand, and immediately the jewels were surrounded by ice.

"What is he doing?" Rachel asked, confused.

"The light and heat of the jewels' magic makes them difficult for cold creatures like Jack Frost and his goblins to hold," Queen Titania explained.

Now Jack Frost was flying back to his ice castle, carried by a frosty wind. He held the jewels in his arms, but Rachel and Kirsty could see that the ice

around them was already beginning to
melt.

Jack Frost swooped down from the gray
sky and landed in his ice castle. By now,
the ice around the jewels was almost gone.
The jewels glowed, casting shimmering
rays of light into every corner of the icy
room. Goblins came running to see the
gems. They wore sunglasses to protect
their eyes from the light.

"Stand back, you fools!" Jack Frost roared, waving his wand and casting another spell to cover the jewels with ice. But the jewels were still glowing, and the ice began to melt away.

"Look, Master!" yelled one of the goblins. "The fairy magic is melting your castle!"

Jack Frost looked around in rage. Sure enough, water was beginning to trickle

down the icy walls, and there was a huge puddle at the foot of his ice throne.

"Jack Frost's magic is not strong enough to block the power of the jewels," Queen Titania told Rachel and Kirsty.

The girls watched as the goblins began rushing around, mopping up the water as fast as they could. But as soon as they

soaked up one puddle, two more appeared.

"Fine!" shouted Jack Frost, stomping his feet in anger. "If I cannot keep the magic jewels, no one else can have them, either! I will cast a spell to get rid of them." And he raised his wand high above his head.

Lost!

"Oh, no!" Kirsty gasped. She and
Rachel watched in horror as a chilly
blast of wind tore through the ice
castle. The glowing jewels were sent
spinning out of the window, where they
scattered.

"See how the jewels grow larger as

they fall into the human world?" Queen
Titania pointed out. The image in the
pool began to flicker and fade. "Because
they are magical, the jewels will hide
themselves until we can find them and
bring them back to Fairyland."

The picture in the pool was fading fast.
But just before it disappeared, Rachel
saw one of the jewels, a cream-colored

stone, fall into someone's backyard. Rachel was surprised to realize that she knew exactly whose yard it was!

Queen Titania shook her head sadly as the image vanished. "All of our fairy seeing magic is used up," she said, sighing. "The pool can't show us where all the jewels have gone."

"But I know where one of them is!" Rachel burst out excitedly. "I recognized the yard where it fell!"

Everyone turned to stare at her.

"Are you sure, Rachel?" Kirsty asked.

Rachel nodded. "It was Mr. and Mrs. Palmer's backyard," she explained.

"The Palmers are my parents' friends. I've been to their house lots of times to help my mom babysit their little girl, Ellie."

One of the fairies was so excited to hear this that she whirled up into the air. Her long brown hair streamed out behind her. "I'm India the Moonstone Fairy," she cried, her eyes shining. "And I'm sure it was my moonstone that fell into your friends' backyard!"

The little fairy wore a pretty dress with a fluttery skirt. The dress was white, but every time India moved, Rachel and Kirsty could see shimmering flashes of pink and blue.

On her feet, India wore dainty white sandals.

"You must meet all our Jewel Fairies," said King Oberon as the other fairies crowded around. "Each one is responsible for teaching all the other fairies in Fairyland how to use her jewel's magic." He pointed at India the Moonstone Fairy. "India teaches dream magic, while Scarlett the Garnet Fairy teaches growing and shrinking magic, Emily the Emerald Fairy teaches seeing magic, Chloe the Topaz Fairy teaches changing and transforming magic, Amy the Amethyst Fairy teaches appearing and disappearing magic, Sophie the Sapphire Fairy teaches wishing magic, and Lucy the Diamond Fairy teaches flying magic."

Rachel and Kirsty smiled at all the Jewel Fairies. "We'll do our best to get your jewels back," Kirsty said.

"Thank you," the fairies replied.

"We knew you would help us," Queen Titania said gratefully. "But Jack Frost knows we will be trying to find the jewels, too. He has sent his goblins into the human world to guard them."

"The goblins will have trouble picking up the jewels," King Oberon continued. "The bright light and magic of the gems will burn them, because goblins belong to the cold, icy world of Jack Frost. Instead, the goblins will probably hide near the jewels and try to keep us from getting them back."

Rachel and Kirsty nodded. They weren't eager to see the goblins again, but they had to help their fairy friends!

Queen Titania looked serious. "So we not only need your help to find each magic jewel," she said, "but to outwit the goblins that are guarding them!"

On the Right Track

"We'll find a way to get the jewels back," Rachel said firmly. Kirsty nodded.

King Oberon smiled at them. "And you will have our Jewel Fairies to help you."

Rachel frowned. "I had a dream that the goblins were chasing me," she said slowly.

India sighed, looking very sad. "Without the moonstone, the fairies' power to send sweet dreams into the human world is fading," she explained. "That's  why you had a nightmare, Rachel."

"India will return with you to your world," said Queen Titania. "She'll help you find the moonstone."

"We know we have to look in the Palmers' backyard," Kirsty said. "But how will we know where to search for the other jewels?"

Queen Titania smiled. "You must let the magic come to you," she replied. "The jewels will find you! And remember, they have grown bigger in the human world, so they will be easier to spot."

Rachel and Kirsty nodded. Then India fluttered over to join them. The Fairy Queen raised her wand.

"Good luck!" called the fairies. Queen Titania waved her wand, and Rachel, Kirsty, and India disappeared in a shower of magic sparkles.

When the cloud of fairy dust had
vanished, Rachel and Kirsty realized that
they were back in Rachel's bedroom.

"We must get to work right away,
girls!" called a silvery voice.

The girls turned and saw India perched
on top of Rachel's mirror.

"Yes, let's go over to the Palmers' house now," said Rachel eagerly. She headed for the door.

Suddenly, Kirsty burst out laughing. "I think we'd better change out of our pajamas first, don't you?"

"Good idea!" Rachel grinned.

"How will we get into the Palmers' backyard?" India asked as the girls quickly got dressed.

"We could throw a ball over the fence," Kirsty suggested. "Then we could ask the Palmers to let us into their yard to find it."

"Yes, that would work," Rachel agreed.

"Girls, are you awake?" Mrs. Walker's voice drifted up the stairs. "Breakfast is ready."

India fluttered across the room and hid  herself in Kirsty's pocket, and the girls hurried downstairs. "Mom," said Rachel as she and Kirsty ate toast and cereal, "is it OK if we go out to play after breakfast?"

"Sure," Mrs. Walker agreed. "But don't go farther than the park, and be back in time for lunch."

"Thanks, Mom!" Rachel said, getting up out of her chair.

Kirsty did the same. "We need a ball," she whispered as they headed outside.

"There's one in the shed, I think," Rachel replied.

The girls found a tennis ball and headed down the street. Even though it was autumn, it was a warm day. The sun shone down brightly from the blue sky.

I hope my moonstone is safe," India said softly, popping her head out of Kirsty's pocket. "I wonder if there are any goblins guarding it."

"We'll find out soon," Rachel replied, stopping in front of a house with a bright red door. "This is the Palmers' house."

The house was only three doors down from Rachel's, on the corner of the street. Rachel took the ball out of her pocket, slipped around the corner, and tossed it

over the fence into the backyard. Then she joined Kirsty and India again in front of the house.

"I'll knock on the door," Rachel said, leading the way up the front steps.

"Let's hope they're home!" replied Kirsty.

Rachel rang the bell, but everything was quiet for a while. Just as the girls and India were starting to give up hope, the door opened.

"Hello, Rachel," said Mrs. Palmer, smiling. "And this must be Kirsty. Rachel told me she was having a friend visit this week."

"It's nice to meet you," Kirsty said politely.

"Sorry to disturb you, Mrs. Palmer," Rachel said, "but I'm afraid we just lost our ball in your backyard."

Mrs. Palmer smiled. "As a matter of fact, I was just sitting out back with Ellie. I didn't see your ball. Do you want to come and look for it?"

"Yes, please," Rachel replied. "If you don't mind," added Kirsty.

Mrs. Palmer opened the door wide. "Go right through, girls. I'm just going to run upstairs for a minute. Ellie's in her stroller on the patio, if you want to say hello."

Rachel led Kirsty through the kitchen and out the back door.

India popped her head out of Kirsty's pocket. "The moonstone is here somewhere," she cried happily. "I can feel it!"

"It's a big yard," Kirsty said. "We'd better start looking right away."

She and India hurried over to the nearest flowerbed and began to look through the shrubs. Meanwhile,

Rachel went across the patio to say hello to Ellie. But as she walked toward the stroller, Rachel began to shiver. Suddenly, there was a chill in the air.

A loud wail came from the stroller as Ellie started to cry.

Ellie must be feeling the cold, too! Rachel thought. *But it was warm just a minute ago!*

Waaah!.....

Mrs. Palmer rushed out of the house and ran over to the stroller. "It's very strange, Rachel," she said. She pushed back the shade and bent down to pick up the baby. "Ellie's always had trouble sleeping. Then yesterday, we got this mobile for her stroller, and she's been sleeping so well." Mrs. Palmer frowned, lifting Ellie out from under her blanket. "Something seems to be upsetting her today, though. She's been restless all morning."

As Mrs. Palmer picked up Ellie, the baby stretched out her chubby little hand to grab one of the decorations hanging from the mobile. Rachel looked at the mobile more closely. It was hung with silver stars, yellow suns, and pale moons. And then, suddenly, her heart skipped a beat. There, glittering in the middle of the mobile, was a cream-colored stone that flashed with pink-and-blue light.

The moonstone! Rachel thought excitedly. *No wonder Ellie's been sleeping well. She must have had extra-sweet dreams!*

"I'm going to take Ellie inside, but feel free to keep looking for your ball," said Mrs. Palmer. "I don't want Ellie to catch a cold. It's a little chilly all of a sudden."

I hope that doesn't mean that some of Jack Frost's goblins are nearby, Rachel thought.

As Mrs. Palmer turned to go inside with Ellie, Rachel ran across the grass

toward Kirsty and India. They were searching around the birdbath in the middle of the yard.

"I found the moonstone!" Rachel whispered triumphantly. "It's hanging in the middle of the mobile on Ellie's stroller."

"Wonderful!" India gasped.

"Way to go, Rachel!" added Kirsty.

"Mrs. Palmer's taking Ellie inside," said Rachel. "We can get the moonstone as soon as she's gone."

The girls and India watched as Mrs. Palmer carried Ellie into the house. Then Rachel and Kirsty immediately ran toward the stroller. India flew along beside them. But before they reached it, the door of the garden shed crashed open, and two green goblins rushed out!

The Big Chase

"The moonstone is ours!" one of the goblins yelled. "We'll never let the fairies have it back!"

"Never! Never!" shouted the other goblin.

As Kirsty, Rachel, and India watched in horror, the second goblin jumped up onto the stroller and grabbed the mobile.

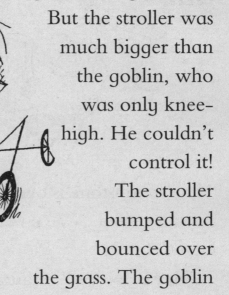

"He's going to take the moonstone!" Rachel gasped. "Stop him!"

As the girls rushed toward the stroller, the other goblin panicked. He rushed to push the stroller away from the girls.

But the stroller was much bigger than the goblin, who was only knee-high. He couldn't control it! The stroller bumped and bounced over the grass. The goblin inside was caught off-balance! With a screech of rage, he tumbled over and got tangled in the baby's blankets before he could grab the moonstone.

Kirsty, Rachel, and India chased after the goblin as he charged across the grass, pushing the stroller in front of him. They could see the moonstone swinging wildly on the mobile, but they couldn't reach it. The goblins were too far ahead!

The stroller jolted along, while the goblin inside struggled to free himself from the tangle of blankets. He shouted at his friend to stop, but with no luck.

Then, all of a sudden, one wheel hit a large stone lying in the middle of the yard. The stroller was moving so quickly that it flipped over! Both goblins let out

cries of alarm as they flew through the
air. They landed in a heap underneath a
large pine tree, covered by Ellie's
blankets.

"India, can you keep them from
getting away?" Kirsty panted as she and

Rachel ran across the
yard toward the
goblins.

"I only have a little
dream magic left. It
might be enough to
put the goblins to
sleep," India replied.

She flew ahead of
the girls and hovered over
the goblins, waving her
wand. A few sparkles of fairy
dust drifted down. The goblins
stopped struggling to free themselves and
began yawning and rubbing their eyes
instead.

"I'm so tired!" one of them said with
a sigh.

"And this blanket is really warm and cozy," the other one said sleepily. "I think I might take a little nap."

"Me, too," the first goblin agreed. "Sing me a lullaby."

"No, *you* sing a lullaby!" the second goblin demanded.

"No, YOU!" yelled the first.

"They're waking themselves up with

their silly argument!" Rachel exclaimed. "What are we going to do?"

"I think I have an idea!" Kirsty whispered. Without saying anything else, she hurried toward the goblins.

Rock-a-bye, Goblins

Rachel and India watched as Kirsty walked right up to the goblins and began to tuck them into the blankets.

"Now, now, settle down," she said in a soft, sweet voice. "It's time for your nap."

The goblins stopped arguing and started yawning again.

"I *am* sleepy," the first goblin mumbled, snuggling down under the pink blanket.

But the second goblin was trying hard to keep his eyes open. "Isn't there something we were supposed to do?" he asked.

Rachel hurried over to help Kirsty. "Go to sleep now," she said in a soothing voice. "You can worry about that later."

Then Kirsty began to sing a lullaby to the tune of "Rock-a-bye, Baby":

"Rock-a-bye, Goblins, under a tree,
out in the backyard, sleeping with glee.
When you wake up from your little nap,
you'll find that India has her stone back."

By the second line of Kirsty's song, both goblins were snoring loudly.

"Nice job, Kirsty," Rachel said with a grin. "But we can't leave the goblins here for Mrs. Palmer to find!"

"Leave that to me," India chimed in. She waved her wand over a

large branch of the pine tree. Immediately,
the branch drooped lower, so that it
completely covered the sleeping goblins.

"Perfect!" Kirsty declared. "The goblins
are green like the leaves, so they'll be
well hidden until they wake up."

India and Rachel laughed.

"Then they'll have to go back to Jack
Frost and tell him they lost the

moonstone," India said. "They'll be in big trouble!"

Chuckling quietly, the girls picked up the stroller and pushed it back to the patio. Then, as India watched happily, Kirsty carefully took the moonstone from the middle of the mobile. It flashed and gleamed in the sunlight.

"We can't ruin Ellie's mobile," India said. She waved her wand, and a glittering, shiny bubble appeared in place of the moonstone.

As it caught the light, it sent rainbow colors sparkling in all directions.

"And now," India went on, "the moonstone is going right back to Fairyland and Queen Titania's crown, where it belongs!" She touched her wand to the jewel. Immediately, a fountain of

sparkling fairy dust shot up into the air. The moonstone vanished. "Thank you, girls," India said, grinning at Rachel and Kirsty. "I must go home now, but I hope you can help the other Jewel Fairies find their magic jewels, too."

"We'll do our best!" Rachel promised.

"Good-bye, India!" Kirsty added as their fairy friend flew away in a cloud of sparkles.

"I wonder where the six other jewels are hiding," Rachel murmured.

"And I wonder if we'll have to face many more goblins," Kirsty said with a frown.

Rachel shivered, remembering her nightmare. "I just hope I don't dream about them again tonight," she said.

Kirsty laughed. "Don't worry, Rachel," she told her friend. "India has the moonstone back now. And you helped her find it. She's sure to send you sweet dreams!"

The Jewel Fairies

India has her moonstone back.
Now Rachel and Kirsty must help

Scarlett the Garnet Fairy!

A Walk on the Farm

"Time to get up!" Rachel Walker called, bouncing on the end of her friend Kirsty's bed. Kirsty Tate was staying with the Walker family during their school break, and Rachel didn't want to waste a single second.

Kirsty yawned and stretched. "I just had the best dream," she said sleepily. "Queen

Titania asked us to help the Jewel Fairies find seven stolen gemstones from her magic crown, and . . ." Her voice trailed away and she opened her eyes wide. "It wasn't a dream, was it?" she asked, sitting up in bed. "We really *did* meet India the Moonstone Fairy yesterday!"

Rachel nodded, smiling. "Yes, we did," she agreed.

Kirsty and Rachel shared a wonderful secret. They were friends with the fairies! They had had all sorts of wonderful adventures with them in the past — and now the fairies were in trouble again.

Mean Jack Frost had stolen the seven magical jewels from the Fairy Queen's crown. He had tried to keep the jewels for himself, but their magic was so powerful that his ice castle had started to melt. In a rage, Jack Frost had thrown the jewels far away, and now they were lost.

King Oberon and Queen Titania had asked Rachel and Kirsty to help return the jewels to Fairyland. The day before, the girls had helped India the Moonstone Fairy find the magic moonstone. There were still six jewels left to find! The girls had to keep looking. But where?

 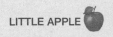

A fairy for every day!

The seven Rainbow Fairies are missing! Help rescue the fairies and bring the sparkle back to Fairyland.

When mean Jack Frost steals the Weather Fairies' magical feathers, the weather turns wacky. It's up to the Weather Fairies to fix it!

Jack Frost is causing trouble in Fairyland again! This time he's stolen the seven crown jewels. Without them, the magic in Fairyland is fading fast!

Look for The Pet Fairies— Coming soon!

■SCHOLASTIC

www.scholastic.com

FAIRY